Pal the Pony

Pal Goes to the Fair

For Betina, who knows just what Pal looks like.
— R.A.H.

For Jade Maddison
— B.O.

ISBN 0-439-68118-9

Text copyright © 2004 by R. A. Herman.
Illustrations copyright © 2004 by Betina Ogden.
All rights reserved. Published by Scholastic Inc.
SCHOLASTIC and associated logos are trademarks and/or registered trademarks of Scholastic Inc.

12 11 10 9 8 7 6 5 4 3 2 1   4 5 6 7 8 9/0

Printed in the U.S.A.
First printing, November 2004

Pal the Pony

Pal Goes to the Fair

by R. A. Herman
illustrated by Betina Ogden

SCHOLASTIC INC.
New York   Toronto   London   Auckland   Sydney
Mexico City   New Delhi   Hong Kong   Buenos Aires

Everyone at the Star Ranch is busy.
They are getting ready for the big county fair.

Bob the bull eats lots of hay.

Fran the hog takes a bath.

Samson the horse is brushed.
Pal the Pony watches.

Pal has never been to the county fair.
He wonders why everyone is so busy.

"Come on, Pal," says Billy.
"It is time for us to get ready for the fair."

Billy gives Pal a bath.

Billy brushes Pal.

Billy combs Pal's tail.

He even braids Pal's mane.
"You look great, Pal," says Billy.

And they ride off to the fair.

There are so many people at the fair.
There are so many animals at the fair.
Pal stands still and looks around.

"Come on, Pal. You do not need to be afraid.
The fair is fun. You will see."

Pal sees the rides.

Pal sees the games.

Pal gets a special treat.

"It is time for the contest, Pal," says Billy.

He walks Pal over to a great big tent.

There are so many animals . . .

pigs, dogs, ducks, chickens, goats,
sheep, cows, and horses.

"All the horses,
come into the center now," calls a man.
"Okay, Pal. Let's go," says Billy.

But Pal sits down.
He does not want to go.
He is too shy.

Billy tries to pull Pal.
But Pal won't move.

"Come on, Pal. *Please*," says Billy.
But Pal won't budge.

Just then, a big horsefly bites Pal on the nose.

Pal jumps up.

He runs into the center of the tent.

Pal gets there just in time.
The judges are giving out the prizes.
Blaze is the fastest horse.

Kicker is the best bucking bronco.
Samson is the strongest horse.
Pal wants a ribbon, too.

Pal is the smallest horse.
Pal is proud of his big blue ribbon.
Pal likes the county fair.